THE
FIELD TRIP

ATTACK ON EARTH

THE FIELD TRIP

R. T. MARTIN

darbycreek

MINNEAPOLIS

Darby Creek
A division of Lerner Publishing Group, Inc.
241 First Avenue North
Minneapolis, MN 55401 USA

For reading levels and more information, look up this title at www.lernerbooks.com.

The images in this book are used with the permission of: llaszlo/Shutterstock.com; briddy_/iStock/Getty Images; ilobs/iStock/Getty Images; 4khz/DigitalVision Vectors/Getty Images.

Main body text set in Janson Text LT Std 12/17.5.
Typeface provided by Adobe Systems.

Library of Congress Cataloging-in-Publication Data

Names: Martin, R. T., 1988– author.
Title: The field trip / R.T. Martin.
Description: Minneapolis : Darby Creek, [2018] | Series: Attack on Earth | Summary: Kayla takes the lead when she and her fellow high school choir members are stranded in an airport during an alien invasion, hundreds of miles from home, with little food and no electricity.
Identifiers: LCCN 2017053115 (print) | LCCN 2017061159 (ebook) | ISBN 9781541525849 (eb pdf) | ISBN 9781541525733 (lb : alk. paper) | ISBN 9781541526273 (pb : alk. paper)
Subjects: | CYAC: Survival—Fiction. | Airports—Fiction. | Interpersonal relations—Fiction. | Extraterrestrial beings—Fiction. | Science fiction.
Classification: LCC PZ7.1.M37346 (ebook) | LCC PZ7.1.M37346 Fie 2018 (print) | DDC [Fic]—dc23

LC record available at https://lccn.loc.gov/2017053115

Manufactured in the United States of America
1-44557-35488-2/12/2018

FOR DOUG N.

ON THE MORNING OF FRIDAY, OCTOBER 2, rings of light were seen coming down from the sky in several locations across the planet. By mid-morning, large spacecraft were visible through the clouds, hovering over major cities. The US government, along with others, attempted to make contact, without success.

At 9:48 that morning, the alien ships released an electromagnetic pulse, or EMP, around the world, disabling all electronics—including many vehicles and machines. All forms of communication technology were useless.

Now people could only wait and see what would happen with the "Visitors" next . . .

CHAPTER 1

"Twenty-seven hours."

Kayla felt her jaw drop a little. "Seriously?"

"Yup," Luke said, rolling a pair of dice and moving his piece forward on the board. "Our plane was grounded at, like, nine thirty yesterday morning, and it's twelve forty-five now. That's twenty-seven hours—a little more, actually."

"This is the longest I've ever been in an airport," Kayla said as she scooped up the dice.

"I feel like this is the longest I've been anywhere."

"I've said it before, and I'll say it again," started Maddie, who was sitting to Kayla's left on the carpet. "That was the first and last time

I will go on a plane. Humans were not meant to fly." Kayla and Luke rolled their eyes.

"This doesn't usually happen," Luke said quietly. "I don't know how many times I've flown. This is the first plane I've ever been on that was grounded."

"Yeah," Kayla added. "Besides, how were we supposed to know . . ." She trailed off.

"That aliens would attack?" Maddie finished for her.

The game stopped mid-play as Kayla and Luke both stared at her. "What? That's what happened."

The entire time the three friends had been in trapped in the airport, they'd avoided talking about the events of yesterday morning. There were enough people around them doing that anyway, all of them afraid. Since the power had gone out, no one had any new information—just wild guesses, nothing productive. In Kayla's mind, discussing their fears of what *might* happen was pointless, and no one was talking about what they could *do* yet.

Maddie looked at the board. "You owe me thirty bucks," she said to Kayla.

Kayla counted out thirty dollars in colorful, fake money and handed it to Maddie. "At least we weren't in the air when it happened," she said.

"Agreed," Luke said.

Kayla and her friends had been flying home from a trip for their choir to perform in New York City. It had seemed like a normal morning until the captain had suddenly announced they needed to make an emergency landing. At the time, he'd told them there was nothing to be worried about, but Kayla distinctly remembered noticing the looks of alarm on the flight attendants' faces as they rushed back to their seats. About twenty minutes later, their plane was landing at the nearest airport—McKenzie-Rowe, apparently located in the middle of nowhere.

Once they were on the ground, Kayla and her friends took out their phones to alert their families of the stop. That was when Kayla's mom called her. She'd heard news of something strange going on—lights in the sky at different locations around the world.

They'd only been on the ground for a few minutes when the real trouble started. Their plane had been rolling toward a gate. Kayla had been in the middle of assuring her mom she'd call her again as soon as they figured out what was going on when her phone suddenly went dead. And it wasn't just her phone— everyone else's phone, tablet, or laptop went dark. The plane stopped moving and the lights went out. It seemed as if all electronics were suddenly dead.

There had been an initial surge of panic— people were shouting questions, wondering what was going on. The noise level in the dark plane rose until a flight attendant got everyone's attention. She instructed everyone to exit the plane through the emergency slide.

The slide had reminded Kayla of one she had been on at a county fair when she was a kid. The difference was that at the bottom of that one, her parents had been waiting for her. At the bottom of this one, there was only the concrete of the tarmac and a stranger wearing an orange reflector vest holding out his hand for her to catch.

Everyone was corralled into the small airport. For the first few hours, airport staff told everyone it was only a delay and they'd give out more information as soon as they had any. Kayla doubted that. She figured the airport staff was buying their time until they figured out what was going on.

People continued to ask when the power would come back and when the flights would resume. But Kayla had a feeling that wasn't going to happen anytime soon either. And, even if everything did suddenly come back on, it would be a logistical nightmare to reload all the airplanes with luggage and people. It would take hours, if not days, before everything got organized again. Kayla knew they were going to be stuck at McKenzie-Rowe for a long time.

That was probably the worst part— McKenzie-Rowe Airport. They were only about four hundred miles from her hometown. If they'd been able to continue flying for just forty-five more minutes, they would have made it home.

It was probably best that we didn't keep going, she reflected now. She didn't want to consider what would have happened if their plane had still been in the air when all the computers, the autopilot, and the emergency systems had all suddenly turned off.

She touched the phone in her pocket without thinking about it. After about ten hours, she'd given up on checking it to see if it had somehow come back on. By this point, it seemed like everyone had accepted the power wasn't coming back on—at least not anytime soon. Kayla was glad she'd been able to talk to her mom before everything had happened, but they hadn't gotten a chance to say goodbye.

"Well," Maddie said, bringing Kayla's thoughts back to the present, "I'm bored with this game."

Kayla chuckled. "I got bored with it an hour ago."

They gathered up the pieces into neat piles and put them back in the box. Kayla took it back to the family they'd borrowed it from—other stranded travelers. She thanked them and walked back to join her friends.

They walked through the terminal to gate nine, where their twenty-member choir was camped out with the other passengers from their grounded flight. The choir director, Ms. Pollack, was staring out the window at the motionless planes littered about the tarmac. She clutched her dead phone in front of her as if it were about to turn on any second.

"We're gonna look for some food," Maddie said as they approached her.

Ms. Pollack turned her head. "Sounds good. If you hear anything, come straight back and tell me. I'd like to get us out of here as soon as possible."

"What?" Maddie said. "You don't want to spend another fun-filled day at the McKenzie-Rowe airport and resort? I'm having a blast!"

"Sarcasm isn't going to get us home any faster, Maddie," Ms. Pollack said, turning back to the runway. "Steph, Josh, and Erin went to see if that Italian place by gate three has anything left. Maybe you could go join them."

They nodded and walked away from the gate.

"How about we go anywhere *but* the Italian place by gate three?" Kayla muttered as soon as they were out of hearing distance.

Luke looked at Kayla. "Have we ever discussed *why* you and Steph hate each other?"

"She's just . . ." Kayla struggled to come to just one answer. "She was—I don't—She's just the worst, okay?"

"I love how constructive and specific you are with your criticisms," Maddie said.

"We just don't like each other. That's all."

She noticed Luke and Maddie eye each other, but they didn't say anything else about it. Kayla started walking a little faster.

Food choices had vanished with the electricity. Much of the food in the restaurants was frozen or had to be made with some form of power. Employees had been kind about handing out their perishable foods, but once the power had been out for a few hours, they started abandoning the shops and restaurants. Some of them closed large metal gates at the storefront. Others simply turned the lights off and hung up hastily made "closed" signs. A few seemed to have simply walked out of the stores without a second thought.

For a while, the stranded passengers waited outside the businesses for someone to tell them they could go in and get something to eat. But when that didn't happen, people began going in and grabbing whatever they could. The airport was so small there weren't many security guards. The handful who had stuck around tried to keep some order around the airport, but after more than a day of being stuck like this, they all seemed to have given up.

By now, Kayla didn't see many airport employees at all. She figured that made sense though. Most of them probably lived around here. If it had been her, she would have run home as soon as she could have.

"Let's check that burger place," Maddie suggested.

"Mei went there last night," Luke said.
"She said there was nothing left besides, like,
a few heads of iceberg lettuce and raw burger
meat. She ended up eating candy bars from one
of the newspaper places. They might still have
some chips or something."

"Worth a shot," Kayla said.

When they reached the little shop, they
found it had been pretty picked over. The store
sold mostly newspapers, books, and magazines,
with just a few shelves for snack items beneath
the checkout counter. The only snacks left
were five bags of dill pickle chips and some
room-temperature sodas.

They stared at these options for a moment
before Luke said, "Better than nothing." They
each grabbed a bag of chips and soda and
headed over to sit on some chairs by one of
the gates.

Maddie winced at the scent that came
out as she opened her bag of chips. "There's
a reason these were all that's left. Even
in the apocalypse people don't want dill
pickle chips."

They ate in silence for a few minutes. Luke finished his chips and stared at the bag. "How much food do you think is left in this place?"

"I would guess a lot," Maddie said. "There are plenty of restaurants in here."

"Yeah, but how much food is left that can be eaten raw?" he replied. "We can't cook anything, and the refrigerators shut down, so that food is probably spoiling pretty fast. How much can possibly be left?"

"And what happens when it's gone?" Kayla added quietly. She'd drunk nearly half her bottle of soda already, and her stomach churned as she realized they should probably start rationing their food.

CHAPTER 2

"We'll cross that bridge when and if we get to it," Ms. Pollack said after Kayla told her their concerns. "The odds are good that everything will turn back on before the situation becomes that bad."

"But what if that doesn't happen?" Luke asked, his eyes wide.

"You guys are being paranoid."

Kayla rolled her eyes as she heard the voice. She turned to see Steph and her friends walking over to where they were standing. "Ms. Pollack is right. If we run out of food, they'll just ship more here."

"Using what?" Kayla shot back. "Trucks and planes don't work. How will they get the food here, Steph? Besides, why would they send food here first? If food's getting distributed, it's probably happening in town."

Steph folded her arms across her chest and wrinkled her nose at Kayla. "Someone will figure something out. It's their job."

"Whose job?" Kayla asked. "You really think someone out there has just been waiting for us to get attacked by aliens?"

"Girls," Ms. Pollack tried to intervene.

"Well it's definitely not the job of a high school choir," Steph said back angrily. "Someone *else* will figure it out. You're just making everyone panic. If someone needs a group to sing with perfect pitch, we're the people for *that* job."

"I'm not trying to make anyone panic," Kayla said defensively. "I'm just worried about what happens when the food runs out." She narrowed her eyes at Steph. "And it *will* run out. I'm trying to solve the problem first so that people *don't* panic."

"Girls, stop!" Ms. Pollack shut down the conversation. "Kayla, if it would make you feel better, see if you can find a security guard and ask if there are any updates. I'm sure that they'll tell you someone is already working on a solution. Steph, if you're not worried, fine, don't be worried. But acting snippy is not helpful. We all need to stay calm right now."

"I agree," Steph said, looking right at Kayla. "We should be calm."

"Go find a security guard," Ms. Pollack said to Kayla, Luke, and Maddie, but Kayla could tell she meant, *please walk away from this.* The three of them headed for one of the security checkpoints to see if any guards remained.

"You know, they're probably right," Luke said. "It's hard for me to believe that no one has a plan for damage control."

"Even if there is a plan," Kayla pointed out, "there's no way to communicate with the outside world. It's not like someone can just make a call and request a supply shipment or something."

They reached the security checkpoint only to find that it was empty.

Kayla sighed in frustration. "So much for that . . ."

Then she spotted a man wearing an orange reflector vest. He was fiddling with a mess of wires dangling from a square hole in the wall. He looked to be one of the only employees left in the airport.

"Excuse me," Kayla said. The man turned around and blinked at them. "Do you work here?"

"Yeah, I'm a mechanic." He pulled the shoulder of the vest to one side, revealing a nametag that read *Orlando*. He turned back to the wires.

"So you wouldn't happen to know how much food is left?" Luke asked. "Or if there's more on the way?"

He shrugged. "No, and I'm not sure *anyone* would know." Without looking back at them, he gestured in a circle with the screwdriver in his hand. "This kind of thing isn't exactly standard procedure for anyone. To be honest, I'm a little surprised the food hasn't run out already."

"What?" Kayla said, panic creeping into her voice.

"We're almost out of food?" an unfamiliar voice asked. A man sitting in the nearby waiting area had overheard them. "How much is left?"

Orlando flushed. "I . . . I don't know."

"So we're going to starve?" the man shouted. Within seconds, other people were standing and joining in, asking questions.

The voices came from every direction, getting louder and louder. People were angry, scared, and just getting more so as they worked themselves into a frenzy.

"I'm just a mechanic!" Orlando shouted to them, holding up his hands defensively. But the people weren't listening anymore.

Two security guards pushed their way through the crowd of people. They held out their hands, trying to stop the questions, but more and more people were adding to the panicked surge of noise. It was clear that they didn't have any reassuring information to share.

This is gonna turn into a riot, Kayla thought. "Let's just get out of here," she hissed to her friends.

With people focused on the security guards, Kayla, Luke, and Maddie snuck off down the hallway. They broke into a run, only stopping when they couldn't hear the echo of angry voices anymore. Luke and Maddie slumped into chairs in a deserted boarding area, breathing heavily.

"Well, that was terrifying," Maddie said.

Luke nodded. "I've never seen people so angry before."

Kayla looked back the way they'd come and noticed Orlando, the mechanic, standing near the bank of windows. He must've sneaked away from the angry crowd too. His hands were shoved deep in his pockets, and Kayla could see in the reflection that he was scowling.

While Luke and Maddie caught their breath, Kayla approached Orlando. "Are you okay?" she asked. "That—that wasn't your fault."

Orlando sighed. "I didn't realize things were that bad," he said quietly. Then he shook his head. "That's a lie. I knew things were bad—I just . . . I didn't want to have to deal with it." He looked at her through his reflection and gave a sarcastic smile. "I told myself it's not my job to worry about that. I thought if I just kept fiddling, trying to figure out a way to bring back the power, it would be enough . . ."

"Hey," Maddie said, joining them by the windows. "Like Kayla said, it's not your fault. No one knew how to prepare for something like this." Kayla was surprised to hear Maddie, the sarcastic pessimist of their group, offer comfort to a stranger like that.

Orlando turned around. "I guess," he mumbled.

"Let's not worry about that right now," Kayla said. "Let's focus on figuring out what we can do." She looked at Orlando. "I'm Kayla, and this is Luke and Maddie."

"Is there anywhere near the airport where we can find food?" Luke asked. "A grocery store or something?"

"Closest one's a few miles out," Orlando said. "But I don't think anyone here is itching to walk around outside when the Visitors could show up at any moment. Besides, in a situation like this, my guess is the place has already been emptied."

"Is there anywhere else there might be more food?" Kayla asked.

"You're asking the wrong guy," he replied. "I'm just trying to get something electrical to start working again. I figured I'd start with that keypad back there and work my way up to one of those." He pointed to the dead planes.

Kayla stared out the window, desperately trying to think of a solution, but all she could see were the dead aircraft. Then, something came to her. "Can you get into the planes?"

"Yeah, sure . . ." Orlando said. "If a plane's power goes out, the emergency doors unlock. If I grab a ladder, I could get you into one of those in five minutes. Why?"

Kayla turned back toward her friends. "Let's go talk to Ms. Pollack. I've got an idea." She looked at Orlando. "You're coming too."

CHAPTER 3

"It's not a permanent fix, but it should hold us for another few days." Kayla spoke to Ms. Pollack, but she was aware that others were listening. Several other people who'd been on their flight were still sitting nearby. "Even if we can't eat the frozen meals, Orlando says that a lot of the food stored in the planes is non-perishable."

A woman wearing a flight attendant outfit cleared her throat. "I'd like to help. I can find where the food is stored. We'll just need help carrying everything."

"I don't think it's a good idea." Steph was seated a few rows away. "We have no idea where the Visitors are or what they might see.

What would you do if they spotted you?"

"Run back here." Kayla shrugged. "Or we could sit here, do nothing, and go hungry, if that's what you prefer."

"It's dangerous," Steph spat back. "We've been staying inside for a *reason*. Some evil race of alien freaks is out there, and if one sees you on the ground, it's going to vaporize you or something."

"You think it's safer to just stay inside and run out of food?" Kayla crossed her arms.

The sound of glass shattering cut through the conversation, and everyone snapped their heads toward the hall between gates. A man had just wrapped a towel around his hand and punched through the front of a vending machine. He slowly removed the shards of glass that remained, letting them drop to the floor. Once a big enough hole was open, he reached in and pulled out as many candy bars and bags of chips as he could carry.

"Yeah," Kayla said sarcastically, turning her head back toward Steph. "It's a lot safer in here."

Steph's eyes narrowed, but she stayed silent.

Ms. Pollack looked hesitant. "I can see how it would be worth the risk. But I don't think you kids should be the ones who do it. Why don't we gather any adults who are willing to give it a shot and—"

"Ms. Pollack, I know we were your responsibility during this field trip," Kayla cut in. "But things have changed."

"You're still minors," her teacher insisted.

"But we're not little kids, and treating us like we are will only make things harder. I'm not going to sit on my hands if there's a chance I can be useful. I'm going out there."

"Me too," said Maddie quickly.

She and Kayla both looked at Luke. "Uh," said Luke, "me three I guess."

"Well I'm not going out there," Steph said loudly.

"No one asked you to," Kayla snapped. "In fact I'm sure Ms. Pollack will be thrilled that you're staying put."

Their teacher sighed. "All right, that's enough. Anyone who wants to go can go—but please be very careful and listen to the adults." She gave Orlando an intense look. "Don't let anything happen to these kids."

He nodded solemnly.

A cluster of people, including several other students from Kayla's choir, gathered around one of the gates. Orlando led the way through the airport.

"The hangar has some storage areas that have food for planes in them, but it's farther away, across the tarmac," Orlando said. He walked quickly, forcing Kayla and the rest of the group to jog just to keep up. "We can start with the closest plane—see what's still on it."

When they reached the gate that held the closest plane, Kayla expected them to just go through the jet bridge like passengers usually did to board. Orlando explained that those doors were operated electronically. They would have to go outside, up, and across the wing to enter the plane.

They took a service entrance down from the gate.

Orlando quickly found a ladder and propped it against the wing, instructing two of the other choir members to hold it steady. He, Kayla, Maddie, and the flight attendant climbed up. Using a lever on the outside of the door, Orlando managed to pop it open. The flight attendant went in first, heading straight for the back. Kayla and Maddie followed. Orlando opened a few cabinets and what looked like a fridge, revealing packages of snacks and fruit. There were beverages too.

They formed an assembly line, handing stacks of food to each other, moving it all toward the terminal. As people inside the airport saw what the group was doing, more ventured out and began pitching in. The assembly line got longer and faster. They emptied the first plane, then the second, then the third, gradually moving farther along the tarmac.

Even with their progress, Steph hadn't been completely wrong—Kayla found she didn't like being outside. She kept glancing nervously at the sky and thinking, *Please, please don't let them appear now.* The farther they got from the terminal, the stronger her fear became. She felt very aware of how far she would have to run to get to safety. And it wasn't just her. She saw other people darting their heads in every direction, no doubt looking for the same strange circles of light that she was.

Once they'd emptied all the planes, Orlando led the group to the hangar with the food storage containers. People began wheeling carts of food across the tarmac to the airport. Kayla was one of the last to grab something.

As she picked up a box, she thought she heard something—voices shouting in the distance. She couldn't make out what they were saying. Orlando stepped outside to see what the commotion was.

"Come on!" Orlando came running back into the freezer. "Leave it! We have to go—now!"

Kayla didn't ask why. She already knew what was wrong—it was the Visitors.

CHAPTER 4

Kayla didn't waste any time. She dropped the box and ran toward Orlando. He waited for her to reach him, and together they raced back toward the airport.

People were shouting all over the tarmac, but they were so far away that Kayla couldn't make out what they were saying. In the dark of dusk, she could only make out tiny silhouettes sprinting as fast they could.

She was holding Orlando back. It was obvious he wasn't running at full speed. She was about to tell him to go on without her when she noticed he was watching something over the top of her head.

She shot a quick glance behind her and saw

a circle of pulsing white lights coming through the clouds. They were moving far too quickly to be planes . . . or anything human-made. They were headed right toward the airport.

Kayla pumped her legs faster until they felt like they were going numb. She looked back at the hangar. They'd come a long way, but the airport still seemed farther than she could run.

The lights were getting closer.

She stumbled and felt one foot catch on the other. Before she hit the ground, Orlando's hand grabbed the back of her shirt and righted her, preventing the fall. "Keep going!" he shouted.

The airport was getting closer, but the lights were nearly over them, much bigger and brighter now. *We're not going to make it,* Kayla thought.

"Truck!" Orlando shouted to her. He pointed at a truck with a cylinder on the back, the type that was usually loaded with gasoline.

When they were close enough, Orlando got down on his hands and knees, crawling underneath it. Kayla did the same, just barely getting under as the lights in the sky reached the edge of the tarmac.

They lay on their bellies beneath the truck as the lights slowed and started to hover, moving over the airport at a snail's pace.

The truck was definitely filled with gasoline. The smell was so strong it was making Kayla light-headed. She became painfully aware of how flammable it was. What if the Visitors had weapons and decided to fire on the airport? The truck could blow up at any second.

The lights stopped. They hovered above the gasoline truck, creating an artificial and eerie daylight. Kayla held her breath, anything to prevent the lights from knowing where she was.

As quickly as the ship had shown up, it left. The lights moved slowly at first, then picked up speed and sped off into the distance. Kayla and Orlando stayed under the truck until the lights had completely vanished over the horizon. Even then, they stayed for an additional minute just for good measure.

When Orlando finally nodded to Kayla, they crawled out slowly as if a sudden motion might summon the light back. They quietly hurried toward the airport. A few others came out from hiding beneath planes, service trucks, even inside a luggage cart. Maddie and Luke emerged from inside a shuttle bus as Kayla and Orlando passed.

No one said a word until they were back in the safety of the airport, but once they were inside, the whole building was filled with the sound of people anxiously whispering to one another. Kayla and her friends, along with Orlando, made their way to the gate where Ms. Pollack was nervously pacing back and forth by the windows.

"Oh my god," she breathed as soon as she caught sight of them. "Are you guys all right? I saw what happened."

"We're fine," Luke said. "Really."

Ms. Pollack gave them a quick squeeze before turning to Orlando, who had slumped back into a chair and thrown an arm across his face. He was still breathing heavily.

"You said you would keep them safe!"

"Hey," Orlando panted, "they're back and all in one piece, aren't they?"

"He did keep us safe, Ms. Pollack," Kayla said. "When the lights showed up, he made sure I found a spot to hide."

Ms. Pollack's face softened. She nodded quickly and wiped at her eyes, trying to collect herself. "I'm just glad everyone is okay."

"I hope you're happy." Steph, who had been sitting in a row of chairs behind Ms. Pollack, leaned over the back of her seat to face them. "You put all those people in danger."

"Everyone made it back, didn't they?" Kayla said, exhaustion coming through in her voice. "And we have enough food for a while now."

Kayla collapsed in a chair on the other side of Steph's. "I told you it was too risky to go out there," Steph said. "What if that thing had taken you all?"

Kayla shrugged. "It didn't."

"It could have," she spat back.

"Did you see how big that thing was? It could have vaporized the whole airport if it wanted to," Kayla said. "At least we did something productive instead of sitting here waiting to be rescued."

"Sure, go ahead, play the hero. That's all you really wanted anyway."

Kayla closed her eyes, feeling far too tired to get into a confrontation. "We have the food we needed. If we have to go outside again, we'll deal with that when it happens. Hopefully, we won't have to."

Steph didn't reply, but Kayla heard her angry footsteps on the carpet as she walked away.

Kayla kept her eyes closed and began to doze off to the sounds of everyone around her speaking quietly. That night she slept better than she had since they'd gotten to this airport.

CHAPTER 5

Kayla woke up to bright light behind her eyelids. Her heart immediately started pounding in her chest.

She scrambled to sit up, only to realize it was just the morning sunlight coming in through the airport windows. She felt heat rush into her cheeks as she realized she'd freaked out for nothing. It wasn't the Visitors coming back for them.

She combed her fingers through her hair and glanced around to make sure no one had noticed. But everyone around her was either still asleep or just waking up themselves. Maddie was stretched out across a few chairs with her eyes closed, and Luke was lying on the floor using his backpack as a pillow and a sweatshirt as a blanket.

The mood of the crowd seemed noticeably better. Kayla looked around and saw people happily munching on snacks from the airplanes.

She had just stood up to stretch when a woman walked up to her.

"Are you the girl who first suggested we collect the food from the planes?"

Kayla blinked at her, not really sure what to say. "Uh, I guess. I mean, a lot of people helped."

"I just wanted to thank you. That was an excellent idea."

Kayla felt herself blush. "I'm sure someone would have thought of it eventually."

"Well, you thought of it first," the woman said, smiling. "Smart girl. Please tell everyone who helped that they have our thanks."

As the woman walked away, Kayla spotted Steph and her friends sitting across the waiting area. They'd apparently heard everything the woman had said. Steph made a show of rolling her eyes to her friends.

Kayla chose to ignore her. She walked a few rows over and found Ms. Pollack in a chair with her head propped on her hand. At first, she couldn't tell if the teacher was sleeping, but when Kayla got closer, her head popped up.

"Kayla," she said with a tired smile. "Good morning. I'm sure you're hungry. Airport personnel brought all the food to the food court. They're handing it out there."

Kayla turned around to see Luke and Maddie both sitting up and rubbing the sleep out of their eyes. "Breakfast?" she asked them.

"You read my mind," Luke said. Maddie nodded through a long yawn.

A few of the remaining airport employees had volunteered to watch over and distribute the rations of food. They handed each person in line a small pack of crackers, a piece of fruit, and a bottle of juice.

"We need to conserve what we have," the employee said. "It may need to last a while."

Kayla and her friends sat at a table in one of the abandoned restaurants. It wasn't the most filling of breakfasts, but it was a relief to have something to eat at all. They'd forgotten to eat before falling asleep the night before, so they wolfed down the food quickly.

The McKenzie-Rowe airport felt much the same as when they'd entered it—people leaned up against walls or curled up in chairs with a book, just waiting to get out of there. There was one noticeable difference. No one seemed to be sitting near the windows. Apparently Kayla wasn't the only one who was feeling a little jumpy after the Visitor incident last night.

As if reading her mind, Luke asked, "What do we do if the Visitors come back?"

"Stay inside," Maddie said through a mouthful of chewed apple. "I hope they leave again."

"Next time we might not be so lucky," Luke replied.

"There's not much we *can* do," Kayla said. She fiddled with her bottle of apple juice, hoping her friends didn't notice the anxiety in her voice. "Without any information, all we can do is wait."

"We're trapped," Maddie said. "We can't go outside. We can't fight them. We can't even find out if someone is fighting them somewhere else."

They finished eating but were careful not to drink all the juice. They sat around for another half hour before they couldn't stand watching everyone else nervously sitting around. They decided to walk through the entire airport and explore. On their third lap, they found Orlando where they had first met him. He was working on the mess of wires again.

"Any luck?" Kayla asked him as they approached.

He kept working as he answered, "Not so much. I've tried replacing every part of the thing, but it still won't turn on." He looked over his shoulder at them. "You kids ever do that science experiment where you make a potato light up a lightbulb?" They nodded, and he tapped the wall with the screwdriver. "I'm about two minutes away from trying that."

"What happened?" Luke asked. "How did we lose power everywhere like that?"

"Best guess," Orlando said, "an EMP."

"A what?" Maddie asked.

"Electromagnetic pulse," Orlando clarified. "It fries the power. That's why everything shut off at once. It also explains why I can't get anything to start working again."

Before they could ask any other questions, a girl from their choir ran up to them. "You guys need to come back right now," she urged. "People are talking about leaving."

CHAPTER 6

"There's an emergency shelter," Steph was saying to everyone in the choir. "Run by the military. It's twenty to thirty miles from here, but we can make it. It's even in the same direction as home. And if anyone can get us the rest of the way home, it's got to be the military. I think we should go."

Kayla, Luke, and Maddie were standing at the edge of the crowd with Orlando behind them. A few others had stopped to listen too.

Kayla folded her arms and scowled at Steph. She realized it seemed silly—first Kayla wanted to go outside and Steph wanted to stay inside, and now Steph wanted to leave and Kayla wanted to stay put.

But that was just it: Kayla *had* gone outside. She'd experienced firsthand how dangerous it could be. Her instincts told her it was safer for everyone to remain at the airport. Most of them had contacted their families before the power had gone out, so this is where all their families thought they would be.

"Where'd you hear this?" Ms. Pollack asked.

"From some of the people here who are actually from McKenzie. Apparently there's an official military base about a hundred miles away—"

"Yeah, Fort Janson," Orlando said loudly enough for everyone to hear.

"Right," Steph said, nodding at Orlando. "And the military also set aside a site for an emergency shelter near McKenzie, in case of something like this." She paused. "Well, maybe not *this* exactly, but you know what I mean. The fort's probably going to send people to staff the shelter site and take care of anyone who needs help. So," she concluded, turning back to Ms. Pollack, "we should go there."

A man from the small crowd standing with them snorted. "I served in the National Guard and I can tell you, the folks at Fort Janson aren't gonna be bothering to staff that shelter site—they didn't set it up after the flood of '08."

Several others nodded. Steph glared at them. The man walked away, and the rest of the crowd followed until it was just the choir members left.

"Say we do decide to head for this military shelter," Luke spoke up. "How are we gonna find it?"

"I heard that if we follow the highway north, through McKenzie, we should run right into the shelter."

"Hang on," Kayla asked. "What happened to 'Everyone should stay inside, and you're a grandstanding idiot if you want to try something else'?"

"You said it yourself—we need to do *something*," Steph said. "Getting the food out of the planes was putting a bandage on a broken limb. We're going to run out again, and there won't be anything to go get next time." She sniffed. "You're not the only one with good ideas."

Ms. Pollack stood up. "Well, we're not splitting up. We'll put it to a vote. The majority wins. Who wants to stay in the airport?"

Kayla's hand shot up. Ms. Pollack waved her finger in the air as she counted. "Nine," she said.

Kayla felt her heart sink. There were nineteen students in their choir. That's when she noticed that Maddie's hand wasn't raised.

"What?" Maddie said quietly. "We can't stay here. She's right."

"Who wants to go for the military shelter?" Once again, she counted. "Ten. We go for the shelter," the teacher announced. "Gather your things and pack as much food as you can. We'll leave first thing tomorrow morning."

She walked up to Steph, and Kayla heard her say, "Take me to the people who told you about this." They left with Steph leading the way.

The choir kids separated into groups, murmuring to one another. Kayla, Maddie, and Luke settled into some chairs nearby.

"I can't believe you sided with Steph," Kayla said to Maddie.

"I didn't side with Steph," she said defensively. "I sided with leaving the airport. We *are* going to run out of food again. It's just a matter of time, and unless you've got another bright idea that you're not telling us, leaving is the smart decision."

Kayla looked down at the carpet. "I don't want to go outside again. When that ship flew over us, I just . . ." She couldn't bring herself to finish the thought. "I don't want to go outside again," she repeated in a mumble.

She wasn't looking at them, but she knew Luke and Maddie were sharing a glance.

"Hey," Maddie said. "We know you're scared. We're scared too. Everyone is."

"But we need to do whatever it takes to stay safe and get home," Luke added.

"We have everything we need here. What if the power comes back tomorrow?"

"I think we're past that," Luke said. "It sounds like no one knows when it will come back—we don't even know if it ever *will* come back. We have to hope for the best but prepare for the worst."

Before Kayla could come up with a response, Orlando walked over to them. "Think I might be able to tag along with you guys?" said he asked. "My brother lives a few towns over—that shelter site is on the way actually."

"We'll ask Ms. Pollack," Maddie said. "I can't imagine she'd say no. Having a mechanic around who knows the area can't be a bad thing. We are a choir, though. How's your singing voice?"

Orlando chuckled. "Bad."

"We'll work on that. Walk with me, Orlando. I'll teach you how to hit a high C."

Luke looked at his watch. It had stopped with all the other electronics, but Kayla noticed that force of habit made him look at it every so often. "We should probably start gathering supplies. I'll see what they're willing to give out for food." He walked off toward the food court.

Kayla sat in a chair, sulking. The thought of having to go outside again was making her more nervous by the minute. Maddie was right—they would eventually run out of food again. And the longer the power stayed out, the less likely it seemed that it was going to turn back on anytime soon, especially if the Visitors were still flying around outside. Leaving the airport *was* the smart plan, but Kayla still didn't like it. Those things *were* still flying around outside.

And she hated that Steph had been the one to come up with this plan.

They'd been in school together for as long as Kayla could remember, and they'd never gotten along. Things only got worse when they both became interested in choir in the ninth grade. By the time they were juniors, it seemed as if they were competitors in everything. They were both sopranos, so naturally they were both constantly trying to prove who could hit the higher note. Whenever there were tryouts for a solo, they both went after it. And when Ms. Pollack asked for someone to hand out sheet music and one of them volunteered, the other had to find a way to one-up her. Kayla didn't know if their rivalry would ever go away.

CHAPTER 7

Leaving the airport the next morning felt like being part of some kind of gloomy parade. Word had gotten around that a group was heading for the emergency shelter. As they marched toward the security gate at the entrance, people sitting by the gates silently watched them leave.

The moment she took a step outside the building, Kayla scanned the horizon for any sign of the Visitors' lights. The farther the group got, the more paranoid she felt.

"It feels super weird being outside now," Maddie whispered to Luke and Kayla when they were only a few steps beyond the parking lot. "I used to like being outdoors, but this. Is. The. Worst."

"No one's around," Luke said. "It's like everyone's . . . gone."

They walked to the highway that led away from the airport, weaving their way around abandoned cars. Everyone watched the sky and kept mostly quiet, afraid too much noise might alert something above.

After a few hours of walking down the highway, they reached a hill. On the other side, they saw McKenzie, the town. They stopped in a line to look at it.

"Spooky," Maddie said. Kayla couldn't help but agree.

McKenzie wasn't a large town, but it wasn't exactly small either. They could see the whole thing sprawled out in front of them covering a valley between two hills, little buildings at even intervals in a grid marked by roads. Even from this far away, it looked deserted. No cars moved down the streets. No one walked down the sidewalks. There was no city noise, no hum of voices or distant construction, or any noise at all—not even birds chirping.

"If we want to turn back," Ms. Pollack said, "now's the time."

There was a moment of hesitation. No one wanted to make the choice at first. Even Kayla felt torn.

"I vote we keep going," Steph said.

"Anyone else?" Ms. Pollack asked.

A few other students nodded in agreement.

"All right, we keep going," the teacher announced. "If I shout *hide*, you hide. No questions—just find cover as quickly as you can." She took a deep breath. "Let's move."

They started down the hill and into town, with Ms. Pollack walking in front.

McKenzie had been eerie from on top of the hill, but up close, it was downright frightening. The few cars that were on the street were parked at odd angles, crossing the middle of the road into where oncoming traffic should be. Their windows were smashed out, and some had doors still ajar. A few had blown-out tires as well. Some businesses were boarded up, and the ones that weren't only had edges of glass shards where the windows used to be.

Convenience stores, gas stations, even the hardware store had all been broken into and looted, their shelves completely bare.

Although the choir members called out, Kayla only caught glimpses of McKenzie's residents. She saw some people peeking from the sides of windows or doors, but as soon as she looked their way, they dodged out of sight. *It's like being in the old west just before a shootout*, she thought.

"I had no idea it would be this bad," Maddie said.

Luke gestured around him. "Meet humanity without its precious electronics."

"We didn't always have electricity, and things weren't like this," Maddie said.

"Well, what's worse?" Luke shot back. "Never having something to begin with, or having something and losing it?" Kayla noticed that Luke's voice was wavering. She could tell he was more upset than he wanted to let on.

"People are just panicked," Kayla said. "It's not just the loss of electricity. It's the fact that the Visitors might show up at any moment. Everyone's scared out of their minds. You saying you're not?"

"I'm terrified," Luke said. "But it's hard not to be cynical about this. Nothing's even broken. It's all just turned off, and look what happened. The Visitors didn't loot these places. That was humans." He looked around like he was making sure no one else was listening. "People will do whatever they have to in order to survive."

"Will you stop complaining?" Steph, a few steps ahead of them, turned around. "We'll be at that shelter in no time, and everything will go back to normal."

Kayla couldn't help herself from scoffing. "In what universe is it normal for us to be at a military camp?"

"They'll take us home."

"Maybe, but we don't know what we'll find when we get home. You're making a pretty big assumption that everything will be fine. If a town like this," Kayla gestured around them, "is so broken, what makes you think ours will be any different?"

Steph glared at her and picked up her pace again, stomping ahead of them.

Kayla gritted her teeth. "Can you believe her?" she hissed to Luke and Maddie.

They gave each other a look, as if to say who they couldn't believe was Kayla.

"Oh, what now?" she asked.

"Nothing," Maddie said. "It's just . . . do you ever think you might disagree with Steph just for the sake of disagreeing with her?"

"*No*," Kayla snapped. "She's just the worst."

"I actually don't think she's that bad," Luke said. "You've just randomly decided that she has to be your enemy. Like, remember when Steph had spent the summer before sophomore year at a singing camp and you were convinced she did it to annoy you?"

"She *only* talked about it when I was around!" Kayla insisted.

"How could you possibly know whether she talked about it when you *weren't* around?" Luke pointed out.

Kayla groaned and moved to walk next to Orlando. They maneuvered around a couple of

cars that looked like they'd been on the verge
of a fender bender when the power went out.

"Normally," he said, "this street would be
totally jammed up with traffic." He pointed
up and down the road. "It's pretty much the
route everyone takes to get anywhere. Seeing
it deserted like this . . ." he shook his head and
looked down. "It's like my hometown's dead."

"I hope your brother's okay," Kayla said.

"Me too," Orlando replied sadly. "The
town where he lives now is smaller than
McKenzie, so I'm trying not to think about
how desperate the people there might feel."
The look on his face made Kayla regret
bringing it up.

They gave up calling out to the people of
McKenzie. It was obvious no one was going to
help them.

"Whoa!" one of the boys shouted, pointing
between some buildings.

A fireball—huge but very far away—was
rising into the sky. Just as Kayla noticed it,
the sound of the explosion reached them.
She could feel the ground rumble where they

stood. The group ducked and covered their heads. Some gravel shifted and a few shards of glass fell from windows. As quickly as it came, the noise faded.

Slowly, Kayla lowered her hands and looked at where the explosion had come from. Tons of black smoke was rising from the area, billowing into the air and forming its own clouds.

"Was that the Visitors?" someone asked.

"We should find cover!" another shouted. "The Visitors could be—"

"There's no ship," Orlando cut him off. "We'd be able to see the lights. It seemed more like something on the ground—maybe a gas leak caused an explosion."

"They could have landed," someone said.

"We should keep moving," Ms. Pollack said. "We're not going that way, and it looked like it was miles from here."

"I'd suggest we pick up the pace a little," Orlando added.

It took them all afternoon to get across town and up the hill on the other side. By then, dusk seemed only an hour or two away, and the choir was moving more slowly, fatigue starting to take its toll.

After a few more miles of walking, they came across an abandoned gas station along the side of the road. Ms. Pollack and Orlando checked it out, found it empty, and agreed that the group should camp there for the night. She and Orlando would take turns keeping watch.

The choir members settled in, leaning up against backpacks and luggage. They ate an unsatisfying dinner of the packaged snacks they'd packed with them. A few students searched the building for any food that may have been left behind, but they came up empty handed. The place had been cleaned out long before they got there.

Everyone was quiet after eating. Kayla could practically feel the tension in the air.

Then a girl sighed and looked at everyone in the group. "What do we do if the shelter isn't there?"

CHAPTER 8

"It *is* there," Steph said defensively.

"The people we spoke with in the airport seemed pretty certain about it," Ms. Pollack said.

Orlando nodded. "Everyone who lives around here knows about it."

"Have you ever been there?" a girl asked. "Even seen it before?"

"Well, no," Orlando said. "It's only for emergencies. If you go by the site on a normal day you're not going to see anything out of the ordinary. But it was specifically created to be a place for people to gather if a disaster happens. I'm sure the military has set up there by now."

"Then why didn't anyone else come with us?" Luke asked.

Kayla snapped her head toward him. She hadn't expected normally quiet Luke to question the plan. Usually he stayed out of debates and conflicts, but since they'd left the airport, he'd been different.

"Has it occurred to you," Luke continued, "that they may have wanted us to leave so there would be more food and space for them at the airport?"

"We took food anyway," Kayla said.

"Only a couple days' worth." Luke's hands were trembling. "We just left a safe shelter based on the word of complete strangers who think there *might* be a shelter somewhere. Who knows how long we'll be out here . . . or if we'll be able to find the shelter . . . or if it even exists in the first place!"

Other students started chiming in, asking nervous questions about what they were going to do. Ms. Pollack was trying to calm everyone down, but anxiety, paranoia, and an entire day of walking had gotten to them. They weren't listening to her.

Several of their classmates looked to Steph

for answers, asking her what to do. But Steph didn't say anything. She seemed to be stunned into silence as questions kept coming at her. The voices in the gas station rose until Kayla could barely think.

"Stop!" She surprised herself at her own outburst. Everyone else looked at her in surprise too. Kayla licked her lips nervously, then straightened up where she was sitting. "Everyone just calm down. Back at the airport, there was no *right* decision to make, but we couldn't afford to not make any decision at all. Staying put and just waiting to run out of food wasn't a good option. We knew this trip was risky, but we agreed it was worth it, and nothing's changed except our attitude. We need to keep going."

Everyone stared at her for another moment. Then the tension in the air broke. People began whispering in small groups, but at least no one sounded panicked anymore. Kayla locked eyes with Ms. Pollack, who looked relieved. She smiled proudly and nodded at Kayla. She gave a quick nod in return.

Luke looked at her a little sheepishly. "Good pep talk."

She gave him a weak smile. "You feeling okay, Luke?"

He shrugged. "I'll be fine. Sorry. I kind of lost it there for a sec."

"I doubt you'll be the last one," Maddie said. "Everybody's wound pretty tight right now."

"But we'll get through it," Kayla added.

One by one, the students fell asleep. Orlando had first watch. He sat by the front door with his chin propped on his fist, looking outside. Kayla appreciated that he was trying to keep watch, but she wondered how effective of a lookout he would be. She could barely see anything. The moon only provided so much light, and it wasn't enough for her. They'd have to hope the Visitors' ships didn't have a stealth mode.

She tried to fall asleep, but it didn't seem like it was going to happen. Even as tired as she was, her mind refused to turn off. It ran through an endless cycle, listing the possible ways this plan could go wrong. *The shelter might not be there. We could run out of food. Someone could get injured. The Visitors might—*

"Kayla, you awake?" someone whispered.

She opened her eyes to see Steph sitting across from her. "What do you want?" she whispered back.

Steph scowled at her. "I'm trying to say thank you."

Kayla's eyebrows raised in surprise. Steph sighed and leaned back against the shelves behind her. "I guess I sort of panicked back there. People were freaking out. I didn't know what to tell them, and . . ." She paused, and her voice lost its harsh edge. "You managed to calm everyone down, so . . . thank you."

Kayla didn't know what to say. This was the last thing she expected to hear from Steph, of all people. "Well . . . *someone* had to do something," she said a little too harshly.

Steph crossed her arms. "Hey, it's not *my* fault that everyone started freaking out. We knew the shelter was twenty or thirty miles away from the airport. It's not like we were going to get there in one day. Just because people had unrealistic expectations . . ."

"Oh, and assuming that if we just keep walking vaguely north we'll find a magical military shelter with everything we need— supplies and transportation and ways to communicate with the outside world—*isn't* an unrealistic expectation?" Even though Kayla had defended her earlier, she was still frustrated Steph for not thinking things through back at the airport.

"The shelter *will* be there," Steph cut her off, standing up and clearly struggling to keep her voice at a whisper. "We just need to go a little farther."

Kayla grunted and rolled over so that she was facing away from Steph. "You'd better be right."

CHAPTER 9

In the morning, Orlando led the way down remote county roads. He said it would be best to avoid the highways because of the all the dead cars that must be clogging them.

Walking in a loose cluster, the choir kept to the center of the quiet road. By the afternoon, they were surrounded by fields of corn and soy. When they got hungry, they stopped for lunch by a fence where some cows had gathered.

"You really don't understand how much stuff runs on electricity until it's all gone," Luke said, looking at his dead watch again.

"What?" Maddie asked, stuffing a few slices of an orange into her mouth.

"Planes, cars, computers, phones, vending machines, refrigerators, watches," Luke replied. "We kind of took it all for granted."

"I never took planes for granted," Maddie said. "Even if the lights turn back on, I'm never going on one of those again."

"I mean, that was just bad luck. I flew so many times when aliens didn't attack, and everything turned out fine."

"Still," Maddie said. "I think I'm done with the sky."

"Let's just get home," Kayla said. "When . . . and *if* the power comes back, then we can try to get Maddie back on a plane."

"Not gonna happen," Maddie said.

The mood of the group seemed to pick up as they walked. Maybe it was because they hadn't seen any evidence of the Visitors in over a day. Maybe they were just sick of silence and hushed tones. But people chatted more naturally and cheerfully now. Except Steph. Kayla watched her walk in silence. Whenever someone spoke to her, she smiled, nodded, and brushed them off.

Maddie and Luke were on round seventy-three of their game of two-person rock-paper-scissors when Kayla finally decided to speak with Steph. *She actually tried to be decent to me last night*, she thought. *And I was kind of a jerk about it. The least I can do is make sure she's okay.*

"Hey," she said when she'd caught up to where Steph was walking.

Steph eyed her. "What?"

"Sorry I was . . . short with you last night."

"It's fine."

"Are you doing all right?" Kayla asked. "You seem anxious."

Steph looked around before leaning in and whispering, "It's just . . . what if the shelter *isn't* there?"

"I thought you were sure about it."

"I'm sure there was a *plan* to create this emergency shelter in the event of a disaster," Steph said. "But what if they weren't able to get it set up? What if the military went somewhere else?"

For a second, Kayla wanted to scold her.

She wanted to remind Steph that earlier she'd had no trouble steamrolling over everyone else's doubts. It was a little late to start second-guessing herself. Before the words popped out of her mouth, though, Kayla thought about how often her own mind had changed in the last couple of days. Steph's worries weren't a sign of weakness or bad planning—they were just the natural result of being human, being scared, and not wanting to put other people in danger. Even if those instincts were kicking in a little late for Steph, Kayla couldn't blame her for them.

"Don't worry about that," she told Steph. "It won't change the situation. All we can do now is see what we find once we get there."

"Maybe we should turn back," Steph suggested.

"Turning around is probably the worst thing we could do," Kayla said firmly. "We've covered so much ground—if we give up now, it'll be a waste. Look, worst-case scenario, we get to the spot where the shelter is supposed to be, and it's not there." It wasn't exactly the worst-case scenario, but Kayla didn't think bringing up alien abduction would be helpful. "*Then* we can turn back, or head for the next-closest town and see if the situation's any better there. But giving up in the middle of the trip won't do any good. We would just end up back at the airport, wondering if we could've made it to safety if we'd kept going."

Steph didn't look much more at ease, but she didn't snap back at Kayla either.

"You had a good plan," Kayla assured her. "You were right—we couldn't just wait around in the airport. It's easy to stress about what happens if the shelter isn't there, but what if it is? Then you're a hero."

Steph finally looked her in the eye and gave her a small smile. "Thanks."

Kayla nodded and slowed down, allowing Steph to walk ahead while Maddie and Luke caught up.

They continued walking all afternoon, over one hill, then the next. The sun was getting low in the sky, and people were starting to talk about making camp for the night.

"Just one more hill," Ms. Pollack kept saying. "Let's cover as much ground as we can."

One of the girls ran to the top of the next hill and turned around excitedly. "It's here!" she shouted, pointing toward the other side of the hill.

Though Kayla—and likely everyone else—was exhausted, she jogged to the top of the hill to see for herself. There it was on the edge of a cornfield. Dozens of green tents were assembled in a perfect grid, with forest green trucks and jeeps between some of them. There was no question—they were looking at a military camp.

"Oh, thank goodness," Ms. Pollack said, running a hand over her face. "Let's get down there!"

They all started running toward the tents. As they got closer, the students began to slow. Everyone at the front of the group stopped in a line.

As Kayla joined them at the bottom of the hill, her stomach dropped. There was something wrong with the camp. There were no soldiers there—no doctors or nurses either. Not even any townspeople. The place was totally deserted.

CHAPTER 10

"Everyone calm down!" Ms. Pollack was trying to regain control of the choir. The students were calling out and running around the camp, searching for any sign of another person. Some of them had even broken down into tears. "Please, everyone just come back here and sit down! We need to decide what we're going to do."

Kayla stayed close to Ms. Pollack, pulling open the flap of the closest tent. The space inside was bare. No sleeping bags, blankets, or pillows. No personal items. Whoever had been here had clearly packed up and left. And if anyone else was still here, they would have heard the group by now.

It's like they vanished, Kayla said to herself. Then she thought about the Visitors. *Or they were abducted.*

Orlando gathered everyone and brought them back to Ms. Pollack. "This is no time to panic," he kept saying. But Kayla couldn't help thinking that this *was* the perfect time to panic.

Once they were back in a group, Ms. Pollack addressed them. "We have to decide if we want to keep going or head back to the airport."

It was going to be a close vote if they took one. Half the students clearly hated the idea of going back the way they came, but the other half were enthusiastic about it. People started shouting their opinions almost all at once. It got louder and louder until the teacher cut them all off.

"Sleep on it. We're not going anywhere tonight. At least the tents are set up, so we'll stay here until morning, but tomorrow we choose. Everyone pick a tent. That's where you're sleeping tonight."

Maddie, Luke, and Kayla picked a nearby tent and dropped their bags in it.

"You guys want to look around?" Maddie asked.

"Beats staying in here," Luke said.

They walked up and down rows of identical green tents, occasionally poking their heads into one to see if any supplies had been left behind. They didn't find anything. They found Orlando seated on a crate, reading a newspaper that someone must've left behind. The headline read: **UNIDENTIFIED LIGHTS: THREAT OR PHENOMENON?**

"Nobody had any idea what those things were when this went to print," he said as they approached. "There's an interview with some scientist in here. He said they were aliens, but everyone probably thought he was jumping to conclusions at the time." He folded the paper and tucked it into his bag. "Who's jumping to conclusions now?"

"Why save it?" Luke asked.

"It might be the last newspaper ever printed," said Orlando.

"Oh." Luke looked down. "Right."

"What happens if we decide to go back to the airport?" Kayla said. "Would you come with us?"

Orlando shook his head. "I've come this far. My brother's still farther down the road, and I figure I can get there in a day or two. I think you all can handle yourselves on the way back if that's what you decide to do."

"I'm not so sure," Kayla said. "Everyone's about ready to crack."

"Yeah," Luke said. "And there's no way to know where we *should* go. We can't even look up where we are!"

"Sure, you can," Orlando said, pulling something out of his coat. "That store we stayed in last night had a whole rack of maps." He tossed it to Luke. "You know, when I was a kid, we didn't have smartphones to tell us everything. Being out here," Orlando gestured around him, "in the middle of nowhere with all the lights out, it's not so different from when I grew up. No internet, just the world around you."

"Wow," Maddie said dryly. "Did you have to walk to school uphill both ways too?"

"No," Orlando chuckled. "Just one way, and I didn't complain about it."

"Cars worked when you were a kid," Kayla said.

Orlando shrugged. "True enough. You know, I tried to rig up one of the shuttle buses at the airport to run. I could have done it too if the thing weren't so modern. Everything was wired through a computer or switchboard. I would have had to rip most of it out and start from scratch. It would've taken forever and I didn't have all the tools I would've needed for a job that complicated."

Kayla looked off toward where the others were setting up. Behind them, she could see the silhouette of a large truck with an open back designed to transport big groups of soldiers. "What about one of those?" she asked.

"Huh?" Orlando looked at her.

"What about one of the military trucks?" She turned to face him. "The shuttle buses are designed for comfort, right? Military trucks would be designed for efficiency. There's probably a lot less stuff in there that you'd have to rip out or rewire."

Orlando stood up, looking at the truck. "It's still got a battery, but if I can get it running in the first place, all I have to do is . . ." he trailed off.

"Orlando," Kayla said, "do you think you could get one of those trucks running?"

He smiled. "Give me a couple hours."

CHAPTER 11

Orlando got to work on the truck right away while Kayla went back to the tent to get some sleep. She had a much easier time drifting off. Sleeping under canvas, it seemed less like they were stranded and more like they were camping. When she woke up, she actually felt rested.

She found Luke and Maddie outside the tent. They'd split a pack of crackers between them. Kayla noticed several of the others seemed to be sharing food too. She frowned. They would need to find help soon or they would run out of rations.

"City centers," Luke said between bites.

"That makes sense," Maddie said.

"What are you guys talking about?" Kayla asked as Maddie handed her a cracker.

"The Visitors are still here," Luke explained. "We're talking about where they're probably located."

"You know," Maddie continued, "that ship hovered over the airport for a while. Maybe they thought it was a small city from the air?"

"It's like they're . . . monitoring us," Luke added.

Desperate to change the subject, Kayla looked over toward the truck. The hood was up, but Orlando was on his back underneath it, arms reaching up into the engine.

"Have you guys talked to Orlando yet?" she asked.

Luke shook his head. "I didn't want to disturb him if there's even a slight chance he can get that thing running. You hungry? I think I've got a few extra packs of crackers."

"I'm okay," Kayla said. "I'll eat later. I'm going to see if I can help him."

"Someone beat you to it," Maddie said with a knowing smile. Kayla gave her a confused look, and Maddie pointed toward the truck without saying anything else.

Kayla walked up to the passenger side door. "How's it coming?" she asked.

Steph's face popped up over the open hood. "It's getting there."

Kayla stared at her in surprise.

"She's been helping me all night," Orlando said from beneath the vehicle. "We took a break to get a few hours of sleep, but work goes a lot faster when someone's handing me all the tools I need."

"And even faster when the person handing you those tools has learned which ones are which," Steph added jokingly.

"It only took you about an hour." Orlando continued working as he spoke. "That's quicker than I learned when I was helping my dad in his shop."

"How old were you?" Steph asked.

"Seven, but take the compliment."

The girls laughed before Kayla asked, "Do you think you'll get it running today?"

"If all goes well. This is an older truck—it's

not rigged up with all the modern electronics. It's not going to be easy to get it started, but I think I can pull it off."

Kayla felt her heart jump with excitement. If they could get the truck working, they'd be home in a day, two max. She noticed Steph's eyes had dark gray bags under them, and she seemed to be swaying where she stood.

"You should get some rest, Steph," Kayla said. "I can take over the tool management."

"I think I'm okay on tools for a while," Orlando said. "What I do need is oil. This thing's running low."

"Oil?" Kayla said.

"Yeah, motor oil. Can you two try to find some?"

Kayla and Steph looked at each other. She couldn't remember the last time she and Steph actually worked together to do something.

Orlando didn't seem to notice the tension between them. "Check in the other trucks. One of them is bound to have some extra."

"Okay," Kayla said. After an awkward pause, the two walked off together.

They searched three trucks in silence without finding anything, but the fourth had a red can in the back. It was too small to be gasoline. Steph put the nozzle to her nose but pulled back quickly. "Yup, that's oil," she said.

"Great. Let's bring it back."

Steph hopped down from the back of the truck, but she didn't start walking right away. "Kayla, why do you hate me?" she asked.

"What?" Kayla did a double take.

"I said, why do you hate me?" For once, Steph didn't look like she was trying to start an argument. She just looked exhausted.

"Why do *you* hate *me*?" Kayla stuttered back.

"I guess it's because I always thought you didn't like me, and I didn't know why. It's . . . frustrating."

Kayla's eyebrows raised. Hearing it out loud made it sound kind of ridiculous. "I guess that's kind of my answer too."

Steph's tired face twisted—not with anger but with amusement. "Seriously?" she said, shaking her head. "We've hated each other since—what—second or third grade for no reason?" She started laughing.

Kayla couldn't help chuckling a little herself. "I mean, little kids make best friends and worst enemies all the time for silly reasons. I guess you and I just got into the habit of disliking each other and never grew out of it."

"Can we call it even then?" Steph suggested. "Start over?"

Kayla smiled. "I think that's the best idea you've had yet."

They made their way back to Orlando and placed the can next to him. "Perfect!" He slid back under the engine. "Can someone hand me the flathead screwdriver?"

"Get some sleep," Kayla told Steph, heading over to where the toolkit was laid out. "You've earned it, probably more than any of us." Steph gave her a little nod and walked away.

Kayla helped Orlando for the rest of the day, handing him one tool after another. He even taught her how to change the oil of the truck.

It was late afternoon before he slid out from under the truck and said, "Okay, let's see if that does it."

Everyone gathered around the truck. Orlando stood over the engine, propping one foot against the top of a wheel well and the other right up against the windshield. He took off his belt and tied it around something in the engine that Kayla couldn't see, then spotted everyone watching him.

He paused. "This may not work. I just want to put that out there. I don't want everyone getting their hopes up."

No one said anything. Kayla knew their hopes were already up.

Orlando gripped the belt and pulled as hard as he could. The engine sounded like a big lawn mower, sputtering for a second then going dead. Orlando adjusted, gripped the belt again, and pulled. It sputtered a little longer this time, but it went quiet again. Orlando took a deep breath and muttered to himself. She could see the frustration in his face. He quickly adjusted something in the engine. Once more, he pulled on the belt. This time, he pulled so hard he fell off the truck.

The engine roared to life.

CHAPTER 12

"It's a temporary fix," Orlando said to the group. "If it runs out of gas or turns off for some reason, it might not start again. You all saw how hard it was the first time. I don't trust it to restart if it stops."

"That means we should go now," Ms. Pollack said. "How far will it get us?"

Orlando shrugged. "I filled the tank, but I couldn't tell you what kind of mileage it'll get, especially after the changes I made. No electricity means it's eating more gas than it would normally. Also, headlights and turn signals don't work. I doubt even the speedometer will function, but it'll move, and that's all we need right now."

"Then let's go!" the teacher said excitedly. "Everyone in the back."

The choir quickly gathered their belongings and rushed to jump into the truck. There weren't really seats, just two long benches, but there was enough space for everyone and their bags. Ms. Pollack said she'd drive first since Orlando had been up all night. Within a few minutes, they were on their way home.

They drove down county roads, guided by the map Orlando had grabbed from the store. Even out here in the middle of nowhere, they had to slow down occasionally to avoid abandoned vehicles

Kayla watched scenery go by: mostly cornfields and soy fields. Every now and then, they passed a cluster of trees.

More than an hour passed before they reached any sign of civilization—a small town, smaller even than McKenzie. As they drove into it, Kayla saw Orlando breathe a sigh of relief.

"This is my stop," he said to her. Orlando gave Ms. Pollack directions, shouting from the back of the truck into the cab. He led them into a residential neighborhood where they stopped in front of a house. Orlando hopped over the side of the truck but made a point of telling Ms. Pollack to "keep it running."

He was only about halfway up the sidewalk when the door popped open, and a man who looked remarkably like Orlando rushed out and hugged him. Orlando exchanged a few words with his brother before returning to the edge of the truck.

"Time for you all to head on without me."

There was a chorus of "thank you" from the students.

Orlando looked over to Kayla, Steph, Luke, and Maddie. "It was great to meet you," he said. "If you ever find yourselves in McKenzie again, let me know."

"Thank you, Orlando!" Ms. Pollack shouted out the window.

Orlando gave one last wave. The truck started moving again. Kayla and the others waved to him until they rounded the corner and he was out of sight.

From there, they made their way back to

the country roads toward home. Every hour, it felt like they were covering the same ground over and over again—the same fields, the same little packs of trees, the same hills.

Kayla poked her head out the side of the truck near the driver's window. "How's it going, Ms. Pollack?"

"It's going all right, but we're going to need gas soon. There's no way we'll make it home on what we've got, not even close."

Some of the other students heard her, and a buzz of concerned murmurs spread through the truck.

"We'll probably hit a gas station soon," said Kayla in what she hoped was an upbeat voice.

"I doubt gas stations will be functioning," Ms. Pollack replied.

"Maybe we can stop and syphon some from a car," Kayla suggested.

"That's probably a better bet," her teacher agreed. "But this thing runs on diesel, which we can't get from a car. We'll stop at the next freighter truck we see."

Steph moved from across the bench over

to Kayla. "People are getting antsy. We need a distraction, like a game or something."

Kayla shrugged. "We're a choir. Didn't you say something about singing in perfect pitch being our job?"

Steph nodded and laughed a little. "Right." She stood by the cab of the truck and began singing the first few bars of one of their songs. It didn't take long for the rest to join in. That seemed to calm everyone for the time being.

Kayla couldn't focus on the song. She was concerned about the gas. So far they'd only passed cars, which were no use. She was afraid the engine would putter out at any moment. She knew they wouldn't be able to get it started without Orlando.

They drove for a few more miles before Ms. Pollack shouted, "Something coming up!" Kayla squinted at the road ahead. *Is that a road block?* she wondered.

As Ms. Pollack slowed the truck and the obstacle came into focus, Kayla saw that two cars had been pushed onto the road so no one could drive past that point.

Kayla got a sinking feeling in her gut. Something about this felt wrong. But in she knew they couldn't turn back. They hadn't passed any gas stations yet, and they would likely run out of gas in the time it took to find a different route. The truck slowed, and Ms. Pollack pulled up to stop a few yards from the roadblock.

She got out, leaving the truck running. "Some of you come help me—let's see if we can move these cars."

As she watched their teacher and a few other students walk over to the cars, Kayla heard a rustling in the woods off to the right of where the truck was parked. *Is it the Visitors?* she thought nervously. Her heart sped up. "H-Hello?" she called out.

"Hello." A man stepped out of the woods. At first Kayla felt relieved to see it wasn't the Visitors, until she noticed the baseball bat hanging at his side. Several others came lurking out of the woods—a woman holding a knife, a guy gripping a pipe, another holding a wrench.

"Kids, stay in the truck!" Ms. Pollack shouted. She turned to the first man. "What do you want?"

He smiled, and Kayla felt a chill run down her spine. "Nice truck you got there. We could really use it."

Ms. Pollack stood perfectly still. "We're just trying to get home."

The man let out a bark of laughter. "We're *all* trying to get home. We owe you a thank you. You brought us this truck, and now *we're* going to get home a lot faster."

He looked from student to student, his smile growing bigger. "Why don't y'all hop out? That truck's ours now."

CHAPTER 13

"Please, we need this truck." Ms. Pollack stood
between the man and the students standing
with her on the road. Meanwhile, the other
adults were closing in around the back of
the truck.

"I'm afraid we can't let you have it," the
man said. He leaned on the bat, using it as a
kind of cane while he spoke. Something about
his casual demeanor made Kayla more nervous
than if he'd just been threatening them.

"Maybe you can come with us," Ms. Pollack
said. "We're headed—"

"Doesn't look like there's enough room," he
said, eyeing the choir. "Come on. Get out."

Kayla saw the defeat on her teacher's face.

Ms. Pollack looked at the students in the truck and nodded. They stood up and hopped off the back of the truck one by one. Once they were out, the adults started filing in.

The man with the bat jumped into the driver's seat and leaned out the window. "Thank you kindly," he said to the choir, and the people in the back chuckled. With that, the truck made a U-turn and drove back the way the choir had just come from.

They stood in the middle of the road for a bit, everyone stunned by what had happened. Just minutes ago they'd been well on their way home. And now their hopes were crushed. The distance they had to travel felt much longer, their situation much more hopeless.

Kayla broke the silence. "How far are we from home?"

Ms. Pollack was rubbing her temples and looking at the ground. "About a hundred and twenty miles," she said flatly. "Give or take. It's hard to tell exactly where we are on the map."

"How long would it take us to walk?" Steph asked.

"Like three days," Luke said.

"I don't have enough food for three days," one student said.

"Me neither," Maddie said.

"Yeah," another student added, "If I don't—"

"We can't stay here!" Ms. Pollack shouted. The rest of the students quickly stopped talking.

Kayla was surprised at her sudden outburst. She'd never seen Ms. Pollack like this. Kayla had always thought their choir director was incapable of losing her composure. She'd kept her cool through everything that happened, but losing the truck must have been the last straw.

Ms. Pollack continued, "We have to keep moving! If it takes us three days, it takes us three days, but we have to go. Now!" She walked around the cars that were blocking the road, and the students followed.

Just as they had when they left the airport, they walked in a loose cluster. They moved over one hill just to head for the next one. No one mentioned their food situation; nobody needed to. *We all know what a disaster it will be if we don't find some source of food soon*, Kayla thought.

One boy grabbed some corn off a stalk in the field they were walking next to. He pulled the husk back and took a big bite, but quickly spit the kernels out. They were far too hard to eat. Some kids grabbed some anyway.

When dusk fell, they made camp in a barn that looked like it hadn't been tended to in decades. Parts of the roof were gone, and there weren't any doors. They ate some of the little food they had left, and Kayla fell into a restless sleep. When she woke the next morning, it felt as if she hadn't slept at all.

They walked into the afternoon. The scenery never changed. The repetitive landscape made Kayla feel like she was walking on a treadmill. They may have been getting closer to home, but it never *felt* like they were making any progress. She took to looking at the ground as she walked.

Suddenly she bumped into Ms. Pollack's back. The teacher had stopped moving, looking hard at the horizon.

"What's up?" Kayla asked.

She didn't answer, but her eyes narrowed, focusing harder on whatever she was looking at. The rest of the choir had stopped as well.

"What is that?" one of the students asked. Kayla still couldn't see what they were talking about.

All at once, the teacher's eyes went wide, and she darted to the side of the road. "It's a truck!" she said. The fear in Ms. Pollack's voice sent a chill up Kayla's spine. "It's coming this way—everyone hide!"

CHAPTER 14

They concealed themselves as well as they could. Most of the students ran into the nearby cornfields. They crouched low to the ground and waited.

Kayla's heart felt like it was beating a mile a minute. *There's no way they didn't see us*, she thought. *We were a big group of kids standing right in the middle of the road. If we saw them, they must have seen us.*

The rumbling came first. Kayla couldn't see much of the road because of the corn stalks, but she heard the sound of the truck. It was getting closer and louder . . . much louder, too loud. It registered with Kayla that she wasn't listening to one truck—there were many. She imagined the people who'd stolen their truck coming back with others to take the few supplies the choir had left.

The sound got louder and louder until Kayla heard the screech of brakes. Kayla heard a door open and footsteps on the gravel of the road.

"Who's out here?" It was a woman, her voice direct and authoritative. "This is Colonel Amanda Lewis of the United States National Guard. If you need assistance come out now!"

Ms. Pollack snapped up from her kneeling position. "We're here! We're here! Help—we need help!" She rushed out from the corn field.

Kayla slowly stood up. This seemed too good to be true, and she wasn't ready to trust it yet. But she saw her friends moving out of the field, so she followed.

As she came out of the stalks, she saw that the woman was telling the truth. She was wearing the camouflage fatigues of the military, and the trucks behind her were filled with men and women dressed identically.

"We walked from McKenzie to the camp you set up south of here," Ms. Pollack explained to Colonel Lewis.

"We took one of your trucks," Maddie blurted out. "But someone stole it from us."

Colonel Lewis brushed off Maddie's comment. "We left that camp three days ago to assist with a power plant that exploded nearby."

The explosion we saw in McKenzie, Kayla realized.

"Where are you heading?" the colonel asked.

Ms. Pollack explained while the colonel listened without any emotion. Once she'd heard the whole story, Colonel Lewis nodded. She pulled a radio out of her pocket and started speaking into it. "Unit five-one-seven, pull up to me. You're gonna be taking a high school choir home."

Everyone stared at the radio. It had been days since they'd seen working electronics. "Your radios work?" Maddie asked.

"Some of them," Colonel Lewis answered. "We have a number of emergency bunkers with supplies in them. They were protected from the EMP blast."

Kayla felt days of tension evaporate from her body all at once. She'd be home soon, home with her family. Some members of the choir hugged each other while Ms. Pollack thanked Colonel Lewis over and over again.

One of the trucks pulled up to them, and everyone hopped into the back.

Kayla leaned over to Steph, who was sitting next to her. "I suppose we can't blame you for not being able to predict a power plant exploding," she said with a smile.

"You know," Steph said, "between us, this could have gone a lot worse."

Kayla laughed. "Seems like things go better when we can figure out how to work together."

"Just try not to get in my way," Steph teased.

They laughed together as the truck took off. Kayla looked over to Luke and Maddie, who were seated across from her. "We're gonna be okay," she said.

Ms. Pollack leaned back where she

was sitting. "I'm just glad we're finally getting home."

"Not quite the field trip you thought it would be, Ms. Pollack?" Luke asked. She just closed her eyes, and everyone else laughed.

Maddie looked around the truck. "I'd still take this over an airplane any day."

ATTACK ON EARTH

WHEN ALIENS INVADE,
ALL YOU CAN DO IS SURVIVE.

DESERTED

THE FALLOUT

THE FIELD TRIP

GETTING HOME

LOCKDOWN

TAKE SHELTER

CHECK OUT ALL THE TITLES IN THE
ATTACK ON EARTH SERIES

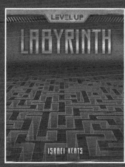

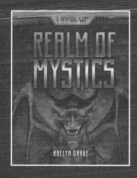

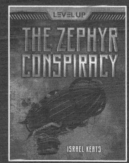

DAY OF DISASTER

Would you survive?

SUPER HUMAN

HAVING A SUPERPOWER IS NOT AS EASY AS THE COMIC BOOKS MAKE IT SEEM.

MIND OVER MATTER

R. T. MARTIN

NOW YOU SEE ME

VANESSA ACTON

PICKING UP SPEED

RAELYN DRAKE

STRETCHED TOO THIN

RAELYN DRAKE

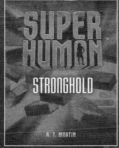

STRONGHOLD

R. T. MARTIN

TAKE TO THE SKIES

R. T. MARTIN

CHECK OUT ALL THE TITLES IN THE SUPERHUMAN SERIES

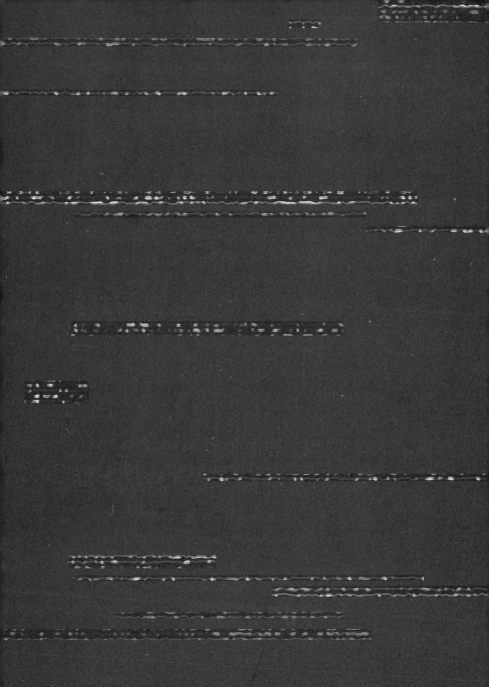